This edition published by Parragon Books Ltd in 2017

Parragon Books Ltd
Chartist House
15–17 Trim Street
Bath BA1 1HA, UK
www.parragon.com

ISBN 978-1-4748-8383-2

Printed in China

# Storybook
# Collection

Bath · New York · Cologne · Melbourne · Delhi
Hong Kong · Shenzhen · Singapore

# Contents

# Pups' Jungle Trouble

Today, Ryder and the PAW Patrol are in the jungle, visiting their friend, Carlos.

"Wow!" says Ryder. "What an amazing place to live!"

"Yes, it is," says Carlos. "It's full of awesome plants and animals."

10

Just then, a loud noise comes from the trees above, "OOH-OOH-OOH-OOH!"

"Talking of animals," says Carlos. "That sounds like Mandy!"

Everyone looks up to see Mandy the monkey swinging towards them.

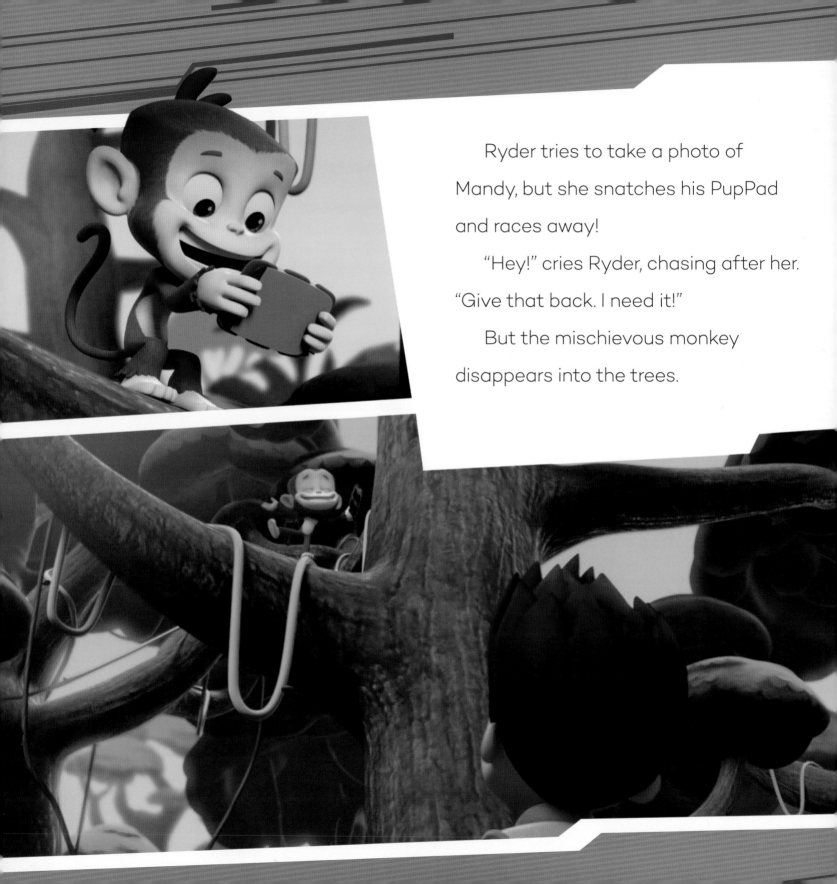

Ryder tries to take a photo of Mandy, but she snatches his PupPad and races away!

"Hey!" cries Ryder, chasing after her. "Give that back. I need it!"

But the mischievous monkey disappears into the trees.

The PupPad tracks Mandy heading out of the jungle and towards some ancient ruins.

"Skye, I need you to find Mandy from the air," says Ryder. "Chase, I need you and your super-spy gadgets to track Mandy from the ground. And Carlos, you can come with me – I need your phone!"

Skye soars over the jungle in her helicopter. She puts on her goggles and soon spots Mandy.

"Ryder," says Skye, calling Carlos's phone. "Mandy's heading towards the ruins!"

**This pup's gotta fly!**

3523.360 6120.820

Ryder, Carlos and Chase zoom up the hill in hot pursuit of the naughty monkey.

"Uh-oh!" gasps Carlos, worried. "These ancient ruins are cursed. Legend has it that once you go in, you never come out...."

"This is the Temple of the Monkey Queen," explains Carlos when they reach the ruins.

"And there's Mandy the monkey!" says Ryder. "She's going in. Let's go after her!"

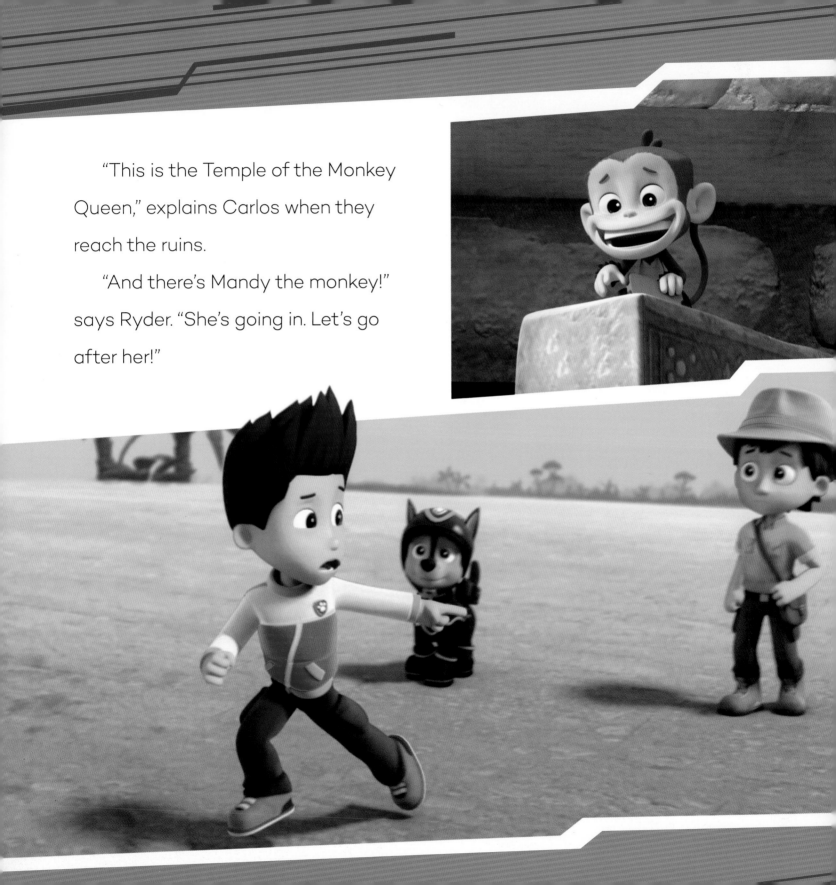

The inside of the temple is dark and scary.

"Light!" barks Chase. He sweeps the room with his torch, looking for Mandy.

"There she is!" says Ryder, spotting the cheeky monkey high on a rock. "Chase, you keep her busy and I'll grab the PupPad."

"Super-spy Chase is on the case!" says Chase. He makes

a zipline and slides along it, trying to distract the monkey.

"Mandy! Watch *this* monkey business!"

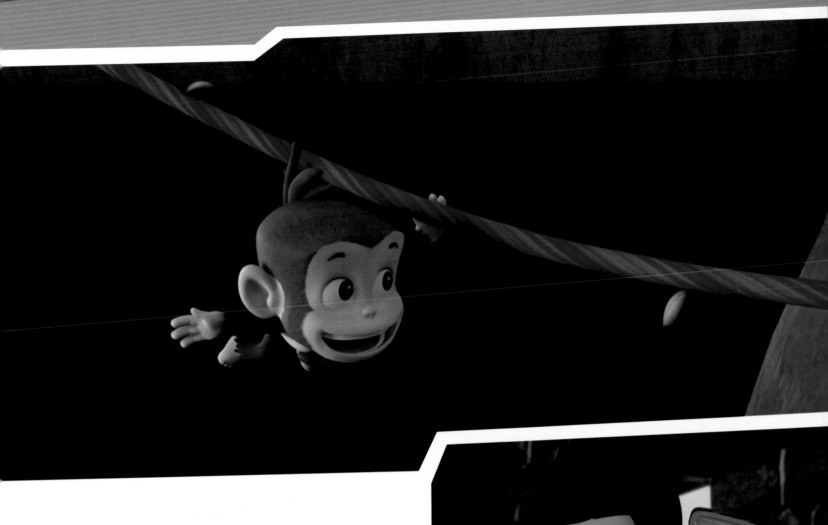

Mandy wants to have a go.
She puts the PupPad down and
zips along a vine.

"Nice move, Chase!" says
Ryder, picking up the PupPad.

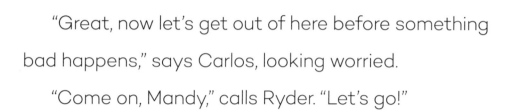

"Great, now let's get out of here before something bad happens," says Carlos, looking worried.

"Come on, Mandy," calls Ryder. "Let's go!"

But Mandy has spotted a gold necklace on a statue. She starts to lift it over the statue's head.

"Noooo, Mandy!" shouts Carlos. "The legend says that if you take the Monkey Queen's necklace, the temple will fall down – with you in it!"

But it's too late. The walls of the temple start to rumble and shake and the statues topple over.

"Let's go!" shouts Carlos. Chase, Carlos and Ryder run for the door, as everything crashes down around them.

When the friends reach the exit,
a statue hits the floor in front of them.
*BANG!* It blocks the door.

Then a boulder falls down and
blocks the door from the outside, too.
The friends push as hard as they can,
but the door won't budge. And the
temple is still collapsing!

Ryder uses the PupPad to call Skye.

"A big boulder fell and is blocking the door out here,"

says Skye. "It's really heavy. I'm going to need help."

Ryder calls Rubble and asks him to bring his jackhammer to the ruins right away.

"Rubble on the double!" says Rubble. He zooms into the jungle and breaks up the boulder.

Back inside the temple, Carlos explains that they need to put the necklace back to stop the walls collapsing.

"Night-vision goggles!" barks Chase. He spots Mandy and ziplines towards her.

Mandy leaps out of Chase's way, but she drops the necklace.

"Now's our chance!" says Ryder. He grabs it and climbs

up to the statue. The temple is shaking all around him.

"Be careful!" shout Chase and Carlos.

"There," he says, placing the necklace

back on the Monkey Queen.

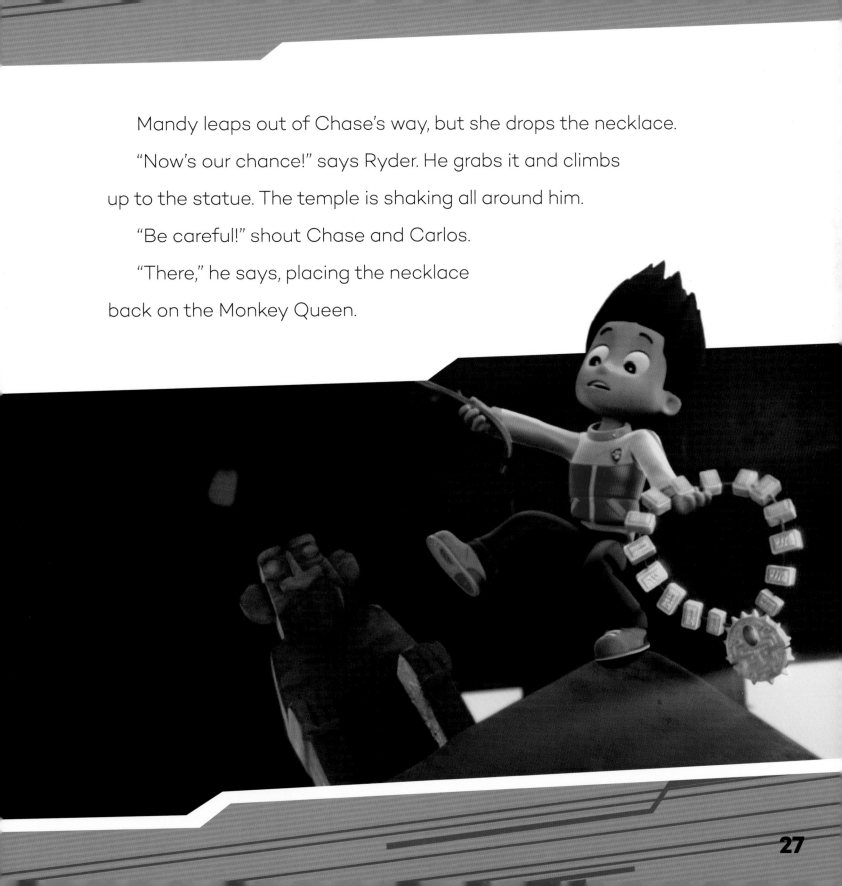

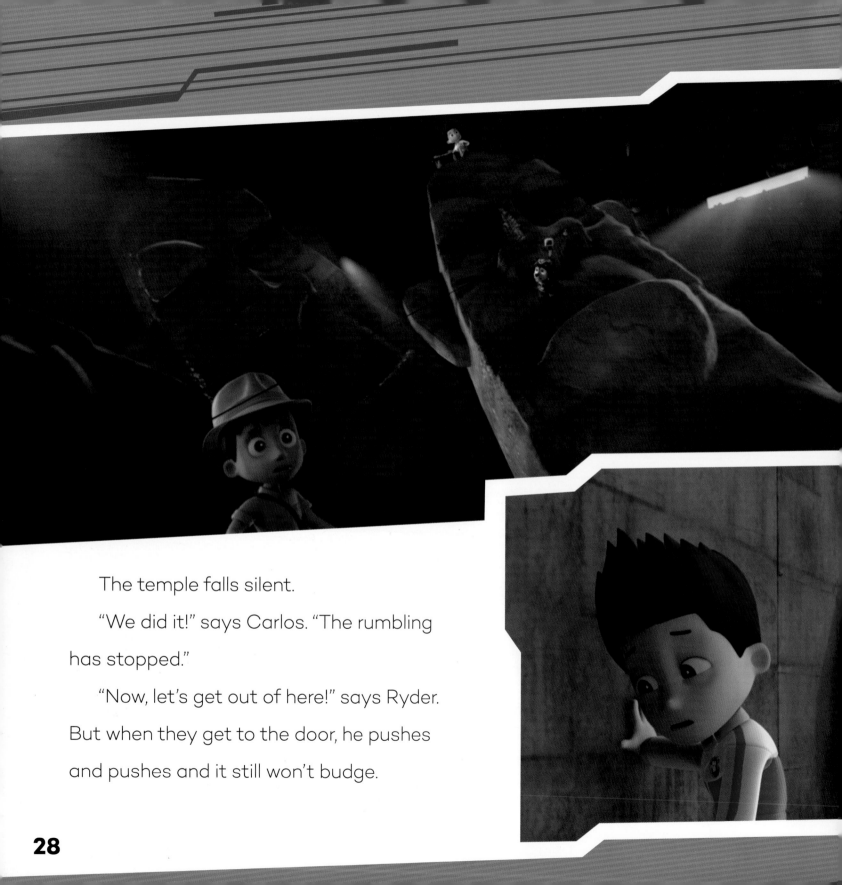

The temple falls silent.

"We did it!" says Carlos. "The rumbling has stopped."

"Now, let's get out of here!" says Ryder. But when they get to the door, he pushes and pushes and it still won't budge.

Suddenly, Mandy jumps on a stone with a monkey carved on it. Slowly, the temple door starts to open!

"Awooo!" howl Rubble and Skye.

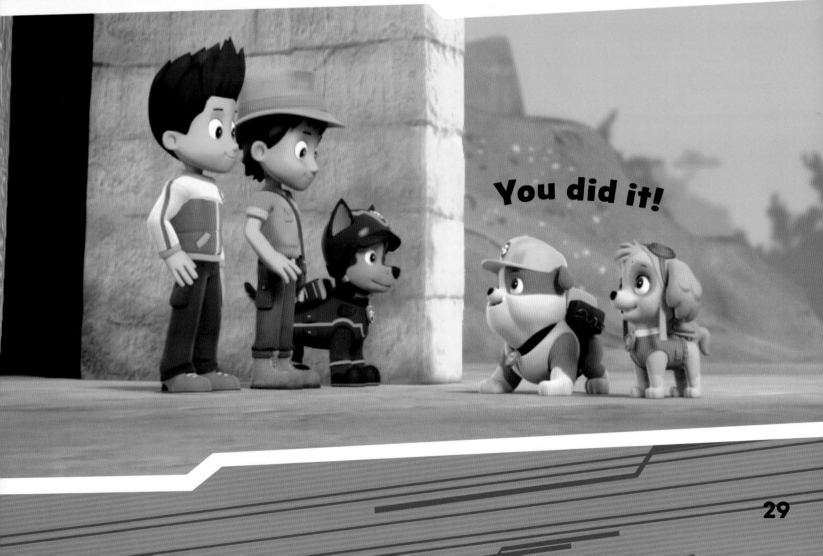

You did it!

That night at the jungle camp, Ryder, Carlos and the pups relax around a campfire.

But Mandy has other ideas. She spots Carlos's phone and swipes it, swinging away through the trees.

"Not again!" sighs Carlos, and everyone laughs.

# Pups Save a Stowaway

Ryder and the pups are getting ready for an exciting trip in the PAW Patroller.

"It's great you're going to help Jake and Everest count penguins," says Katie.

"Yeah," replies Ryder. "The pups are going to love it!"

Meanwhile, Cali wanders off and finds Rocky's catapult. She sniffs it, then hops onto it ... and steps on the release pedal!

"YOWWWLLL!" she cries, flying high up into the air.

YOWWWLLL!

Cali lands in Rubble's digger with a BUMP! Rubble doesn't notice – and scoops her up along with the luggage. He puts the cat and the cases in the back of the PAW Patroller. "Loading up!" he says.

"Okay, pups," says Ryder at the wheel. "We're rolling out!"

"Uh oh," sighs Cali. No one spots her underneath the bags.

As the PAW Patroller rolls through the snow, the pups put on their winter gear.

"Welcome to the land of ice and penguins!" says Jake when they arrive.

The pups are very excited to see the penguins.

"Wow, look at them all!" says Skye.

While the pups and the penguins play, Cali hops out of the PAW Patroller and spots a seagull.

She pounces after it and lands in Everest's snowplough. Her paws accidentally hit some buttons and the plough sets off with a ROAR!

"That's my snowplough!" cries Everest, watching it zoom by. "With Cali driving!"

Just then, Ryder gets a call from Katie.

"Don't worry, Katie," says Ryder. "Cali's here and we'll get her home safely."

"And don't you worry, Everest," adds Ryder. "We'll get your snowplough back, too."

Ryder calls the pups for their help. "Pups! To the PAW Patroller!"

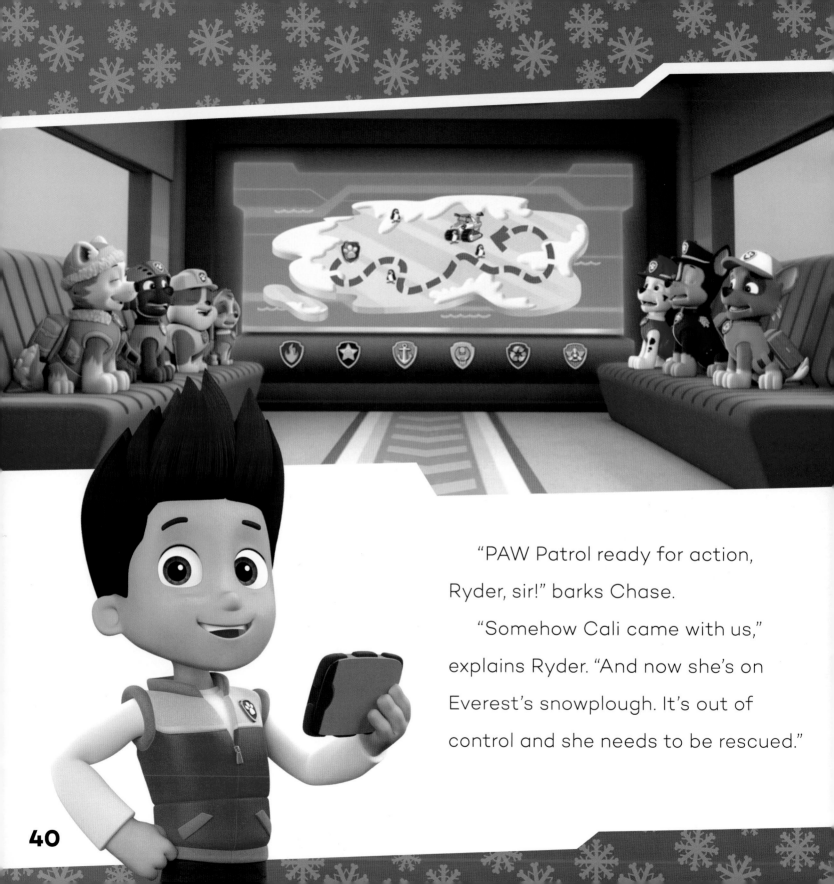

"PAW Patrol ready for action, Ryder, sir!" barks Chase.

"Somehow Cali came with us," explains Ryder. "And now she's on Everest's snowplough. It's out of control and she needs to be rescued."

Ryder asks Skye to track Cali from the air and tells Chase and Everest to stop the runaway plough.

"PAW Patrol is on a roll!" says Ryder.

"Arooooo!" howl the pups, heading off after Cali.

Pups away!

Cali nervously scrambles over the snowplough, pressing more buttons.

*PING!* One button launches the sledge out of the back and some playful penguins hop on board.

WEEEEE!

The speeding snowplough hits a bank of snow and sends Cali and the penguins up, up, up into the air ... and down into the water! Cali is thrown out of the snowplough and lands on a patch of ice.

Meanwhile, the penguins hop out of the water as the snowplough hurtles along the edge of a cliff!

Skye calls Ryder from her helicopter. "Cali's drifting out to sea and the snowplough is running on its own!" she says.

"Okay, Skye," replies Ryder. "We've got this."

Ryder tells Chase and Everest to get the snowplough and then calls Zuma.

"I need you to help me get Cali, Zuma. She's floating on ice out in the water."

"Totally on it, Ryder," replies Zuma.

Chase and Everest catch up with the snowplough.

Everest leaps onto the plough and brings it under control.

"Great jump!" cheers Chase, and they head back to the PAW Patroller.

Meanwhile, Ryder and Zuma are racing across the water and ice.

"These snow drifts are totally awesome!" says Zuma as a penguin jumps on board his hovercraft. "Hold on tight, little dude!"

Ryder and Zuma soon find Cali.

"Jump, Cali!" says Zuma. But she's too afraid to move.

"Can you reach her with your buoy, Zuma?"

asks Ryder.

"Great idea," says Zuma, and he quickly shoots out the buoy and slips it over Cali.

"Nice job, Zuma," says Ryder.

"Hold on, Cali!" calls out Zuma.

"We're heading for shore."

Back by the PAW Patroller, Jake and the rest of the pups are finishing counting the penguins.

"Looks like that's the last of them," says Jake.

"You might want to make a note about this one, Jake," says Ryder, arriving with Cali. "We can study the migration habits of the *wild* Cali!"

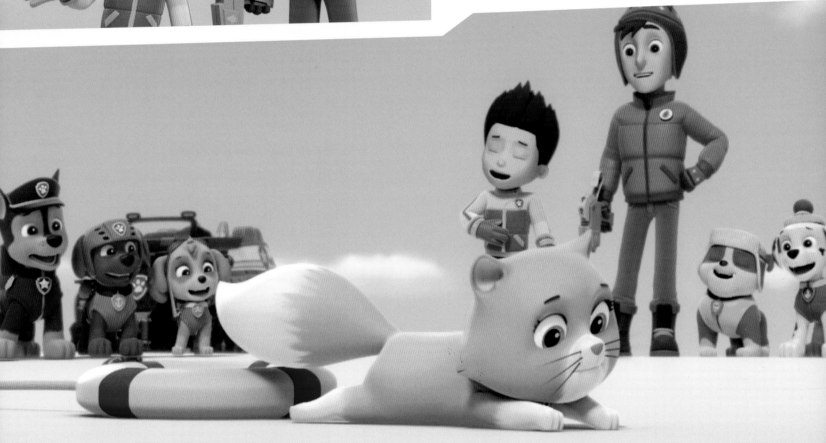

"Cali, you're safe!" cries Katie on the
PupPad. "Thanks, Ryder. Thanks, pups."

"You're welcome," replies Ryder.
"Remember, if you ever need us, just
*squawk* for help!"

"SQUAWK!" chirp the penguins.

# Pups Save a Pool Day

It's a hot and sunny day in Adventure Bay.

Rocky and Rubble are in the park.

"I need to cool down," says Rubble.

"Let's take a dip in the pool!" says Rocky.

Rocky and Rubble head to the pool,
but when they get there, it's empty!

"Oh, no! What happened to the water?"
says Rocky.

"I don't know," says Rubble, "but we have
to find out. This is a job for the PAW Patrol!
Let's go."

Over at the Lookout, Skye and Marshall
are packing things for a day at the pool.
"Are you ready?" asks Skye.

"Almost," calls Marshall. "I just need my towel, sun cream, hat, water and my Super Dog comic book. Now I'm ready!"

Rubble and Rocky race
down Main Street, where they
find Ryder and their friend Alex.

"Hey, pups," says Ryder.
"What's wrong?"

"There's no water in the
pool," pants Rocky.

"No water? What are we going to do?" asks Alex.

"Don't worry," says Ryder, pulling out his PupPad.

"The PAW Patrol will fix it." He hits the alarm button and calls the pups to the Lookout.

The pups line up in the control room.

"The water from the water tower isn't reaching the pool," says Ryder. "We need to find out why."

"Marshall, I need your ladder to check out the tower. And Rubble, I need your shovel in case we need to dig up a blocked pipe."

The pups are excited to help.

"Everyone else, head to the pool!" says Ryder.

Ryder, Rubble and Marshall arrive at the water tower. The pad holding up the tower has slipped, and the water pipe is bent.

"We have to fix the tower before we can fix the pipe," says Ryder. "We just need a few more paws to help us!"

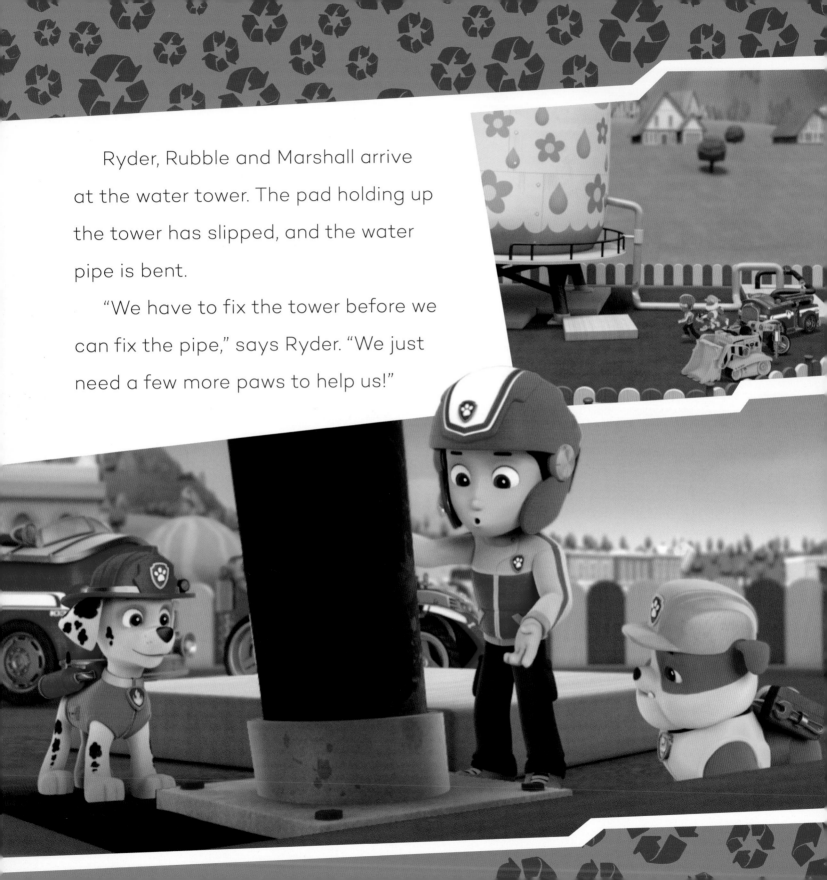

Ryder calls Rocky and Chase. "Chase, we need your winch. And Rocky, we need your forklift, too."

"You got it, Ryder!" bark Chase and Rocky.

When Rocky and Chase arrive at the water tower,
all the pups leap into action.

"Marshall," calls Ryder, "can you climb up your ladder
and attach Chase's winch hook to the tower?"

"Winch cable is hooked on!" says Marshall.

Let's dig it!

Next, Rubble uses his digger to make a pile of earth near the tower.

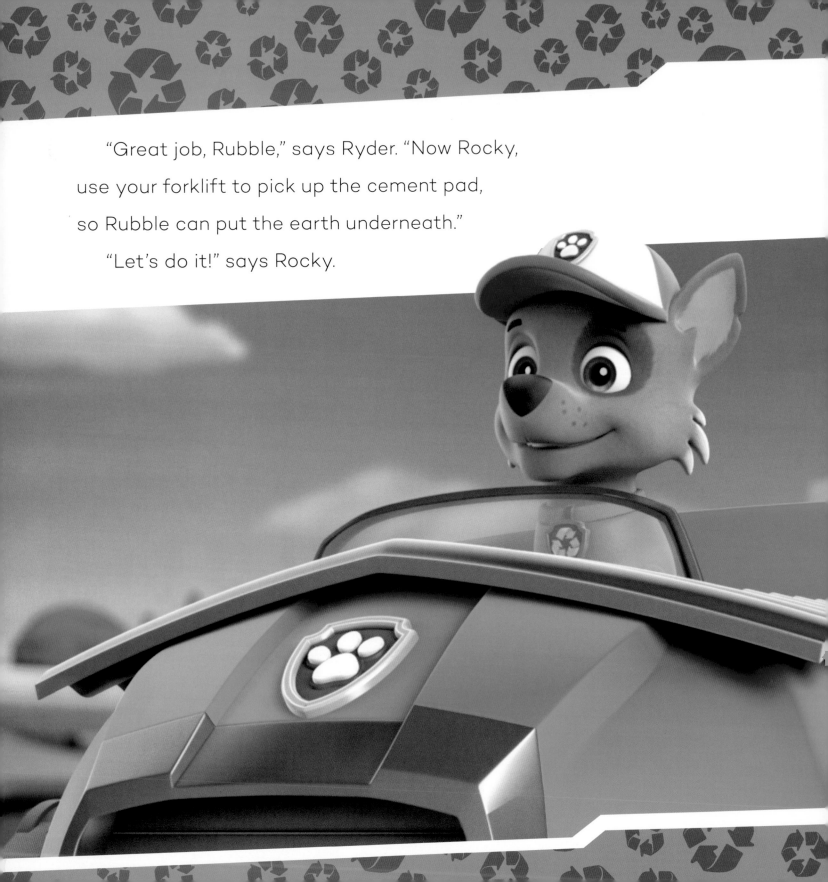

"Great job, Rubble," says Ryder. "Now Rocky,
use your forklift to pick up the cement pad,
so Rubble can put the earth underneath."

"Let's do it!" says Rocky.

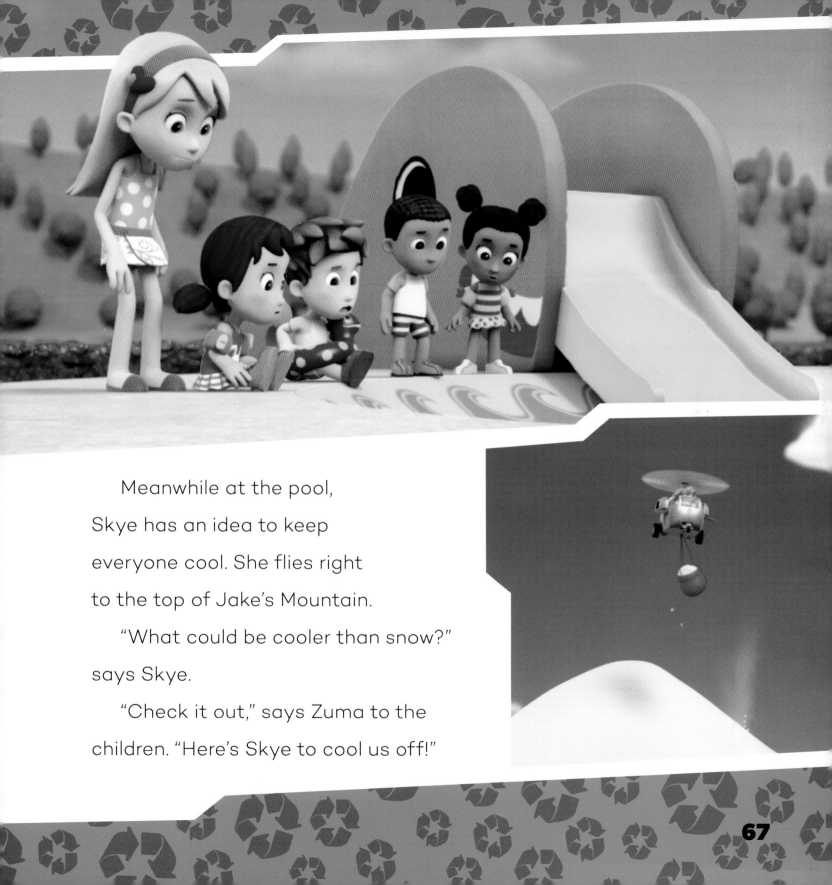

Meanwhile at the pool,
Skye has an idea to keep
everyone cool. She flies right
to the top of Jake's Mountain.

"What could be cooler than snow?"
says Skye.

"Check it out," says Zuma to the
children. "Here's Skye to cool us off!"

But when Skye drops the snow, it all lands on Zuma!

"First I was a hot dog, now I'm an ice pup!" says Zuma.

Back at the water tower, the PAW Patrol are finishing the repairs.

Chase pulls the tower with his winch. Then Rocky lifts up the cement pad and Rubble dumps earth underneath the base.

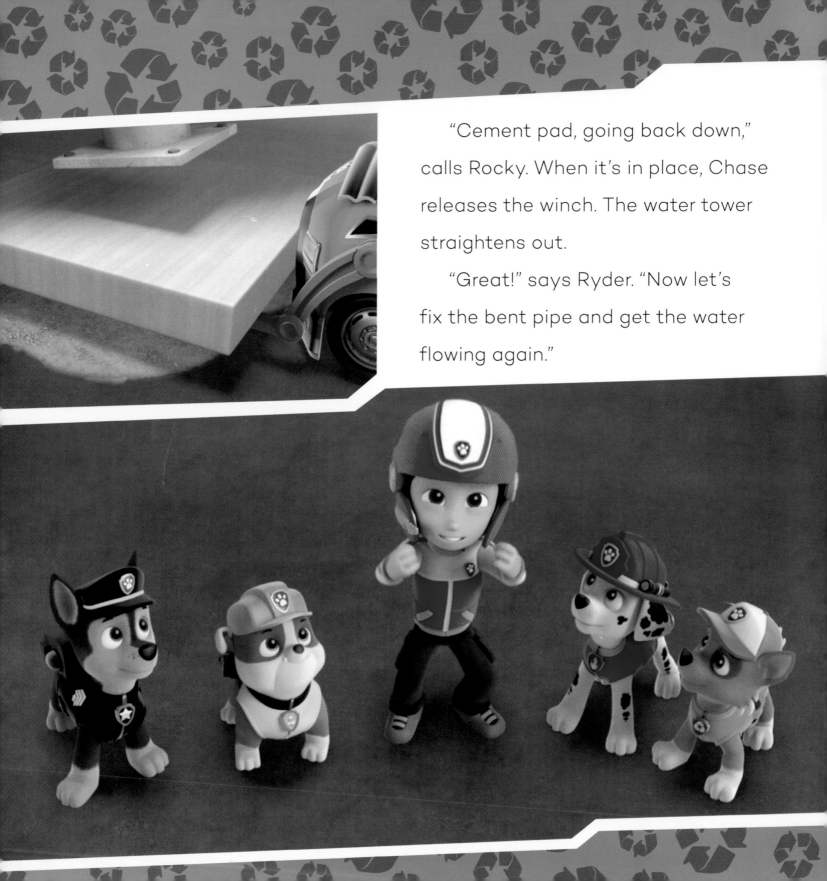

"Cement pad, going back down," calls Rocky. When it's in place, Chase releases the winch. The water tower straightens out.

"Great!" says Ryder. "Now let's fix the bent pipe and get the water flowing again."

Rocky finds a spare pipe in his recycling truck and screws it into place.

"That should do it," says Rocky. "Let's see if we fixed it."

Ryder calls Skye on the PupPad. "Skye, I'm just about to turn the water back on. The pool should start filling up any second now."

"Thanks, Ryder," says Skye. "Get ready, everyone, the water is on its way!"

When the pool has filled up, Zuma says,

"All right, everybody. Ready, set … get wet!"

Ryder and the other pups
arrive at the pool.

"Thanks for fixing the pool,
PAW Patrol!" says Alex.

"You're welcome, Alex,"
says Ryder. "And remember,
whenever there's trouble,
just yelp for help!"

# Pups Save
# the Turbots

Ryder and the PAW Patrol are playing volleyball on the beach.

"Get the ball!" bark Zuma and Rubble.

The pups are soon joined by Cap'n Turbot and his friend.

"Hi, everyone," says the captain.
"This is my cousin, François.
He's from France."

"Ooh-la-la!" says François.
"The only thing better than football
is volleyball. Make room for one more!"

Cap'n Turbot leaves François
to the volleyball game.

"I think I saw a blue-footed booby
bird down by the bay," Cap'n Turbot
tells Ryder. "If I can get a photograph,
it might make it onto the cover of
*Marine-Bird Monthly*!"

"Good luck," calls Ryder.

Wally the walrus pops up and barks loudly. At first Cap'n Turbot doesn't understand but when he looks at where Wally is pointing, he sees the blue-footed booby bird.

"Oh! There it is!" gasps Cap'n Turbot. "On my boat!"

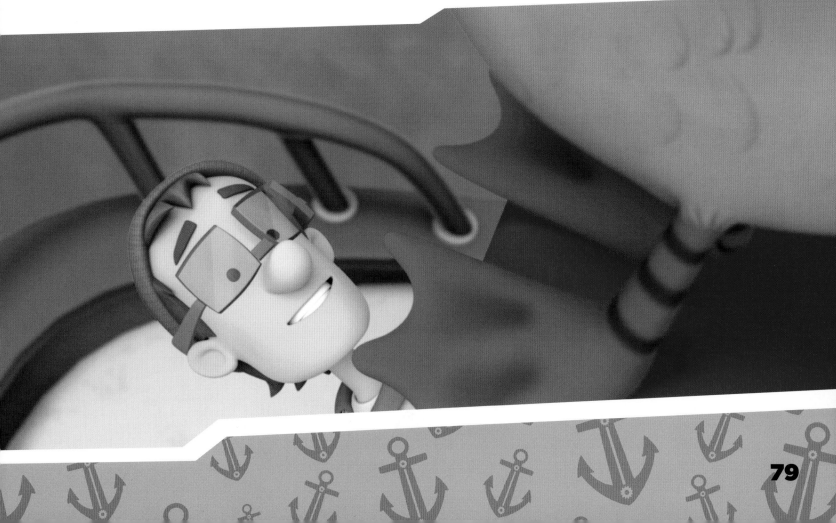

Cap'n Turbot is so busy trying to take a photograph, he falls overboard and scares the booby bird.

"Oh, no! Come back!" cries Cap'n Turbot as the bird flies away.

Ryder and the pups are still playing
on the beach when Wally swims up.

"Hi, Wally," says Ryder. "What's wrong?"

Wally barks, points and flaps his flippers until
Ryder understands the problem.

"It's Cap'n Turbot!" says Ryder. "He found his bird, but lost his boat ... I think Wally is trying to tell us that the captain needs our help."

Ryder pulls out his PupPad. "No job is too big, no pup is too small. PAW Patrol to the Lookout!"

At the Lookout, the pups are ready for action.

"Pups, Cap'n Turbot needs us," says Ryder. "He was trying to take a photo of the blue-footed booby bird, but ended up in the bay."

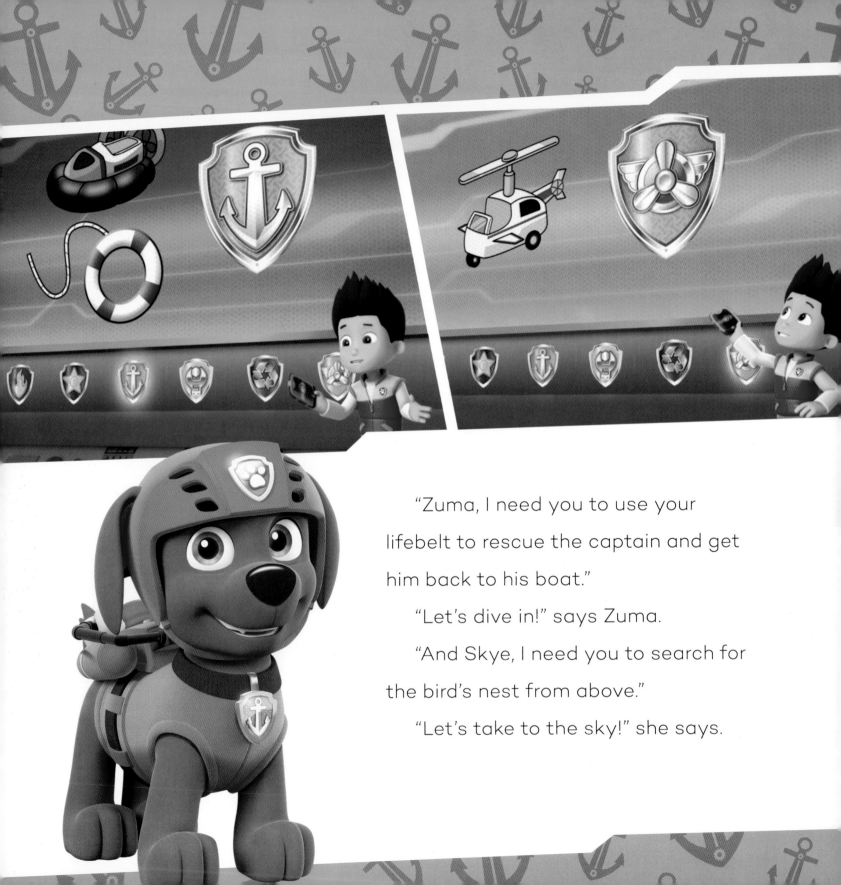

"Zuma, I need you to use your lifebelt to rescue the captain and get him back to his boat."

"Let's dive in!" says Zuma.

"And Skye, I need you to search for the bird's nest from above."

"Let's take to the sky!" she says.

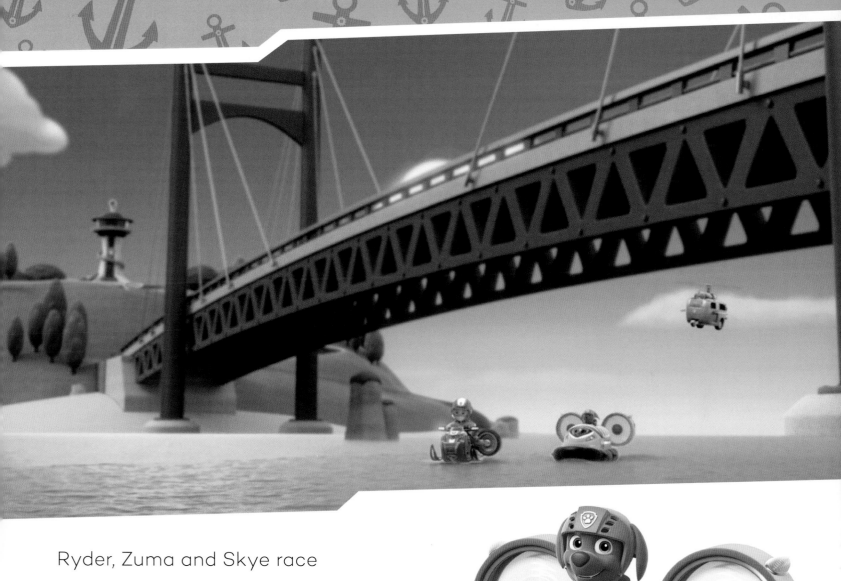

Ryder, Zuma and Skye race
across the bay.

"There he is!" cries Zuma.

"Hang on, Cap'n Turbot,"
calls Ryder. "Zuma will get you –
I'll rescue your boat."

85

Zuma launches the lifebelt.
It lands over Cap'n Turbot and
Zuma pulls him back to his hovercraft.

"Woo-hoo! Thanks, Zuma," says
Cap'n Turbot.

Zuma and Cap'n Turbot climb aboard the Flounder. Ryder and Skye are already there waiting.

"We'll help you get some pictures of the booby bird," says Ryder.

"Thank you," says Cap'n Turbot.

Suddenly, François surfs in, almost knocking over his cousin.

"Okay, Horatio. I will take a picture of this bird for you."

Cap'n Turbot sighs.

Meanwhile, Skye is flying across the bay looking for the blue-footed booby bird. She spots its nest on the cliff's edge.

"That's it!" Skye shouts into her helmet mic. "I couldn't miss those bright blue feet!"

"Bingo!" cries Cap'n Turbot. "You've found it!"

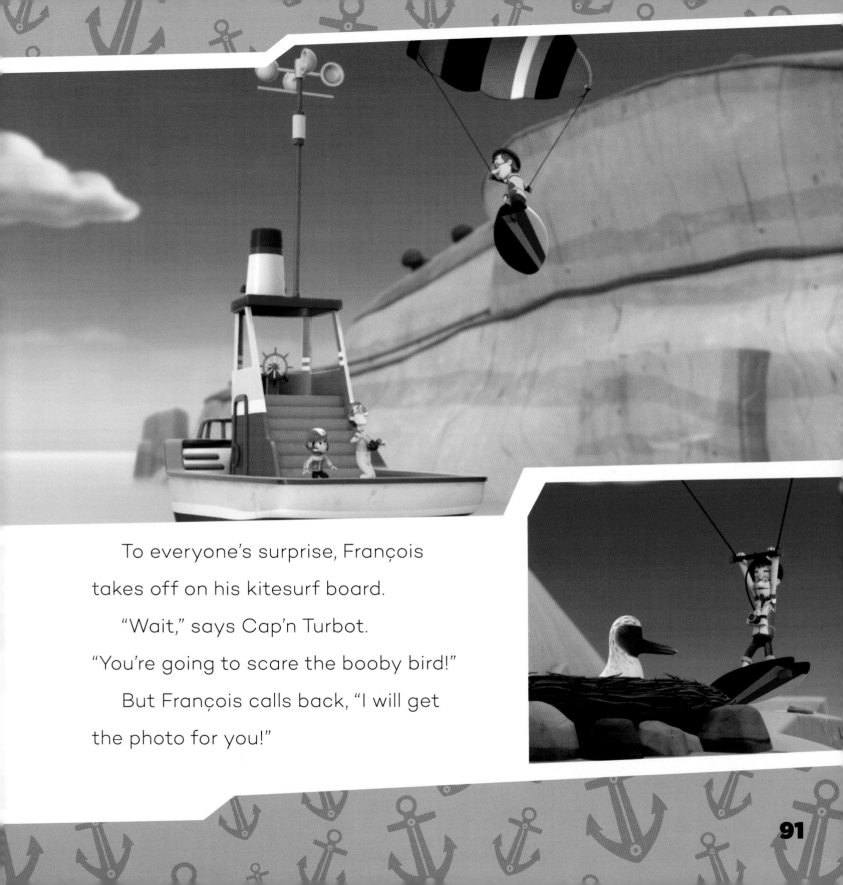

To everyone's surprise, François
takes off on his kitesurf board.

"Wait," says Cap'n Turbot.
"You're going to scare the booby bird!"
But François calls back, "I will get
the photo for you!"

The wind carries François' kitesurf board up to the bird. He gets out his camera.

"Say 'Le Cheese'!" shouts François. The booby bird flies straight at him.

"Mad booby bird!" cries François.

François falls off the cliff edge
and clings on with one hand!

Skye quickly flies over. She lowers
Cap'n Turbot down to François.

"Hang on, François," calls the captain.
"Help is here!"

"Help, Horatio!" cries François. "This is a very angry bird."

The booby bird hops onto François' hand. He lets go of the cliff in fright and lands in the sea.

SPLASH!

The PAW Patrol help François onto the boat and Cap'n Turbot turns to the booby bird.

"Hello, beautiful birdie," says Cap'n Turbot. "Can I take your picture, please?"

The bird poses happily.

Later, at the park, Cap'n Turbot gives Ryder a present.

"I brought you this picture of the blue-footed booby bird to thank you," says the captain.

"Thanks!" says Ryder. "The PAW Patrol is here to help!"

# Pups and the Big Freeze

"Wow! It looks like Adventure Bay froze over last night," gasps Rocky, as he races outside to play with Chase and Rubble.

"Whoaaa!" cry the pups, skidding across the icy ground into ...

... a huge pile of snow!

"It really did freeze last night," says Chase, giggling at their new snow hats.

Over near the bridge, Mayor Goodway and Chickaletta are sliding around on the ice, too.

"Oh, noooo!" cries the Mayor, as her car skates across the icy road and ...

... crashes into a big bank of snow!

"I'm stuck!" says the mayor, trying to reverse out. "I need to call the PAW Patrol."

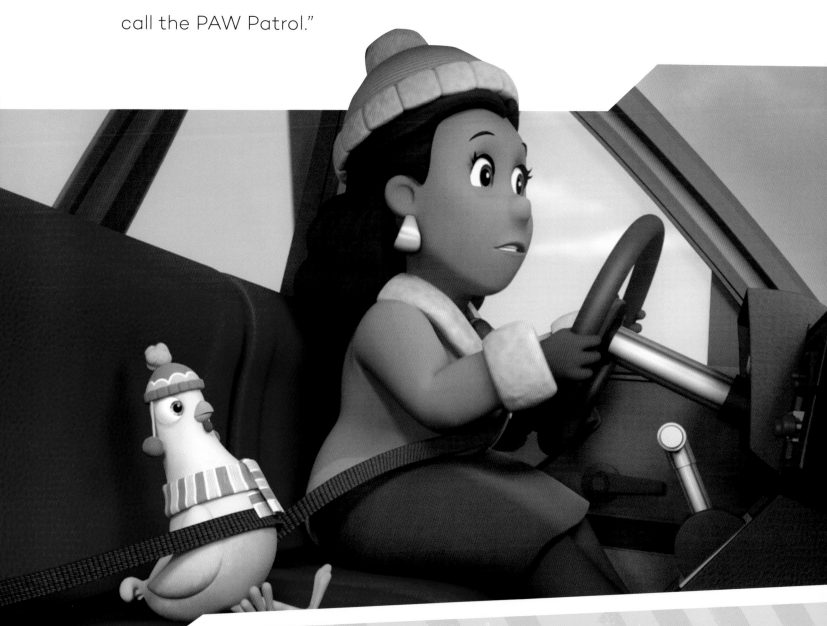

"Ryder," says Mayor Goodway over the phone, "the streets are covered in ice and my car slid into a bank of snow. I can't get out."

"Leave it to the pups, Mayor Goodway,"
Ryder replies. "We're on our way."
Ryder hits the alarm on the
PupPad and says, "PAW Patrol
to the Lookout!"

Let's roll!

"PAW Patrol, ready for action!" says Chase when they arrive.

"Thanks, pups," says Ryder. "Adventure Bay is super-slippery today. Mayor Goodway slid into a snow bank and she needs our help."

Ryder asks Chase to bring his winch, then tells Rubble to clear the roads.

"Rubble on the double!" says the pup, taking the lead and clearing the way with his digger.

"Great job, Rubble," says Ryder when they arrive.

"Chase – it's winch time."

"Chase is on the case!" replies the police pup.

Ryder ties on the winch and Chase starts its motor.

The winch pulls the car out of
the snow.

"Well done, Chase," says Ryder.
"All clear, Mayor Goodway."

"Thank you for rescuing me, Ryder,"
says the mayor.

Just then, Ryder's PupPad rings. It's the train driver.

"Branches are blocking the crossing," he says. "And the train's brakes won't work on the icy tracks!"

"We're on it!" says Ryder.

"I know just the pup to lend a paw,"
says Ryder as he calls husky pup Everest.

"Hello, Ryder. How can I help?" she asks.

"The train crossing is blocked and we have to
clear the tracks," explains Ryder. "Come quickly!"

"The train driver can't stop," explains Ryder when Everest arrives. "And if he hits the branches, the train will jump the track. We have to work quickly."

Leaping into action, Chase and Ryder use the winch to pull the branches off the track.

"Winch hook!" barks Chase.

Next, Everest uses the trail-clearing arm on her snowplough to lift a huge tree trunk and drag it out of the way of the train.

"Great job, Everest," says Ryder.

"Here comes the train. Hurry, Rubble!"

**112**

Rubble pushes his shovel along the tracks, scraping the ice and snow away as fast as he can.

When the train approaches the station, Ryder tells Rubble to pull over.

"He should be able to stop now you've cleared the tracks," says Ryder.

"Fingers crossed his brakes will work."

"Getting off the track on the double!" replies Rubble.

The train driver slams on the brakes and comes to a stop at the station.

*HONK! HONK!*

"Woo-hoo! The brakes are holding," cheers the train driver. "Thanks, Rubble!"

"No problem," Rubble replies.

"We did it!" says Ryder, heading back to the bridge to meet everyone. "Now let's celebrate. Who wants to skate?"

"I was born to slide!" howls Everest, and she and the rest of the pups race off to play.

"This will help you slide, Everest!" cries Marshall. "Water cannon!"

The fire pup shoots a stream of water that instantly freezes into a solid arch in the cold air.

Whoooaaa!

"An ice slide!" says Everest, scrambling to the top. She zooms down so fast that she bumps into Zuma and Skye at the bottom.

The pups go flying up, up, up ... and straight into a pile of snow!

"Hee, hee, hee!" everyone laughs, looking at their silly snow hats.

"What a good bunch of pups," says Ryder.

# Pups Save the Parade

The pups are getting their vehicles ready for the Adventure Bay Day parade.

"Your pirate-boat float looks great, Zuma!" says Chase. "And Skye, your skywriting helicopter is …"

"... in pieces! Oh, no. Can you finish putting it together in time for the parade?" asks Chase.

"Nearly finished," says Ryder.

"And then this pup's gonna fly!" says Skye.

Meanwhile, on Main Street, Alex is helping Katie with her pet-bath float.

He ties on so many balloons that they lift the bath up into the air!

"Maybe that was too many," says Alex, as the bath floats away with Cali and Chickaletta inside.

Katie, Alex and Mayor Goodway chase after them, but the bath floats higher and higher until *BUMP*! It gets caught on top of the lemonade stand.

"What should we do?" asks Mayor Goodway.

"I know," says Alex. "Let's call the PAW Patrol!"

Mayor Goodway quickly takes out her phone. "Ryder, we need your help!"

126

"No job is too big, no pup is too small," says Ryder, pushing a button on his PupPad. "PAW Patrol to the Lookout!"

Marshall, Rocky and Zuma race to the Lookout as their pup tags light up.

"Katie's float is stuck and Cali and Chickaletta are inside," Ryder tells the pups. "Marshall, I need you to use your ladder to bring them down, and Chase, I need you to keep the area clear."

When they arrive, Chase uses his
megaphone and traffic cones to clear
the area and make a safe space for the
bath to land.

"Everyone, please keep clear!"
calls Chase.

Marshall drives his fire engine
to the lemonade stand and
climbs up his long ladder.

"Cali! Chickaletta!" he calls.

"I'm here to get you down safely."

Ruff-ruff
rescue!

But as Marshall reaches for Chickaletta, the bath wobbles and Cali jumps on his face.

"Woah! I can't see!" cries Marshall, tumbling into the bath and knocking it free of the stand.

As they float away, the bath hits the City Hall tower with a *THUMP*! Poor Chickaletta tumbles over the side.....

"Net!" shouts Chase from the ground, quickly shooting out a net from his pup pack to cushion Chickaletta's fall.

The chicken bounces off the net straight into Mayor Goodway's arms.

"You're safe!" cries the mayor, happily.

Back up in the air, the bath is still caught on the tower, but it has tipped off balance. Marshall is hanging off the edge with Cali holding on to his tail!

"Hello!" Marshall calls. "I could use some help!"

Ryder pulls out his PupPad. "Skye, I need you to get Marshall and Cali down from the bath float. Hurry!"

"On my way, Ryder," replies Skye. "I've just finished preparing the helicopter."

**Pups away!**

"Let's take to the sky!" says Skye, heading off to find Marshall.

"Skye!" calls Marshall, seeing her approach. "Boy, am I glad to see you."

Skye dangles a harness in front of Marshall. "Grab on!" she calls out.

The crowd gasps as Marshall leaps off and grabs the harness bar with his teeth. Skye flies Marshall and Cali away from the bath and lands them safely on the ground.

"You're safe," says Chase.
"And right between my cones!"

Cali jumps into Katie's arms.
"Cali! I'm so glad you're okay,"
Katie cries.

"But what about the
floating bath?" says Marshall.

Chase fires tennis balls into the air, popping the bath's balloons one by one. Slowly, the bath floats back down to the ground.

"Thank you so much, Ryder," says Mayor Goodway.

"And thank you, PAW Patrol!" adds Katie.

"No problem," replies Ryder.

Now everyone is safely on the ground and the floats are ready, the Adventure Bay Day parade can finally begin.

"PAW Patrol – to your floats!" shouts Chase through his megaphone.

"WOW!" gasps the Adventure Bay crowd. The floats look amazing!

"Hooray for Adventure Bay Day and hooray for the PAW Patrol!"